Whales and Other Creatures of the Sea

A Random House PICTUREBACK®

With thanks to Dr. Daniel Odell of Sea World, Orlando, Florida, and to Paul Sieswerda of the New York Aquarium

 Published in the United States by Random House, Inc., New York, and simultaneously in Canada by Random House of Canada Limited, Toronto.

Library of Congress Cataloging-in-Publication Data:
Milton, Joyce. Whales and other creatures of the sea / by Joyce Milton ; illustrated by Jim Deal. p. cm. — (A Random House pictureback) Includes index. SUMMARY: A tour of the sea from the shore to the darkest depths, focusing on such animal inhabitants as the blue whale, manta ray, jellyfish, angler, and tube worm. ISBN 0-679-83899-6 (pbk.) — ISBN 0-679-93899-0 (lib. bdg.). 1. Marine fauna—Juvenile literature. [1. Marine animals.] I. Deal, Jim, ill. II. Title. QL122.2.M56 1993 92-2409 591.92—dc20

Manufactured in the United States of America 10 9 8 7 6 5 4 3

Whales and Other Creatures of the Sea

By Joyce Milton Illustrated by Jim Deal

Random House New York

Oceans cover most of our planet earth.

People go to the seashore to swim and play. Children run up and down the beach looking for pretty shells. Sometimes they see crabs scuttling across the sand. They may even find a starfish.

For other people, the ocean is a place to find good things to eat. In the shallow water, a man and a woman are digging for clams. A fishing boat returns to dock loaded with silvery fish.

When the fishing boat leaves the harbor again, gulls fly after it. Dolphins swim along with the boat too. Farther out, the fishermen see a whale. When the whale breathes, a jet of spray shoots high into the air. Suddenly the whale leaps up. Seconds later it is gone.

Whales and dolphins live in the water, but they are not fish. They breathe air through a hole in the top of their heads. They are mammals—relatives of land animals like cows, horses, and dogs.

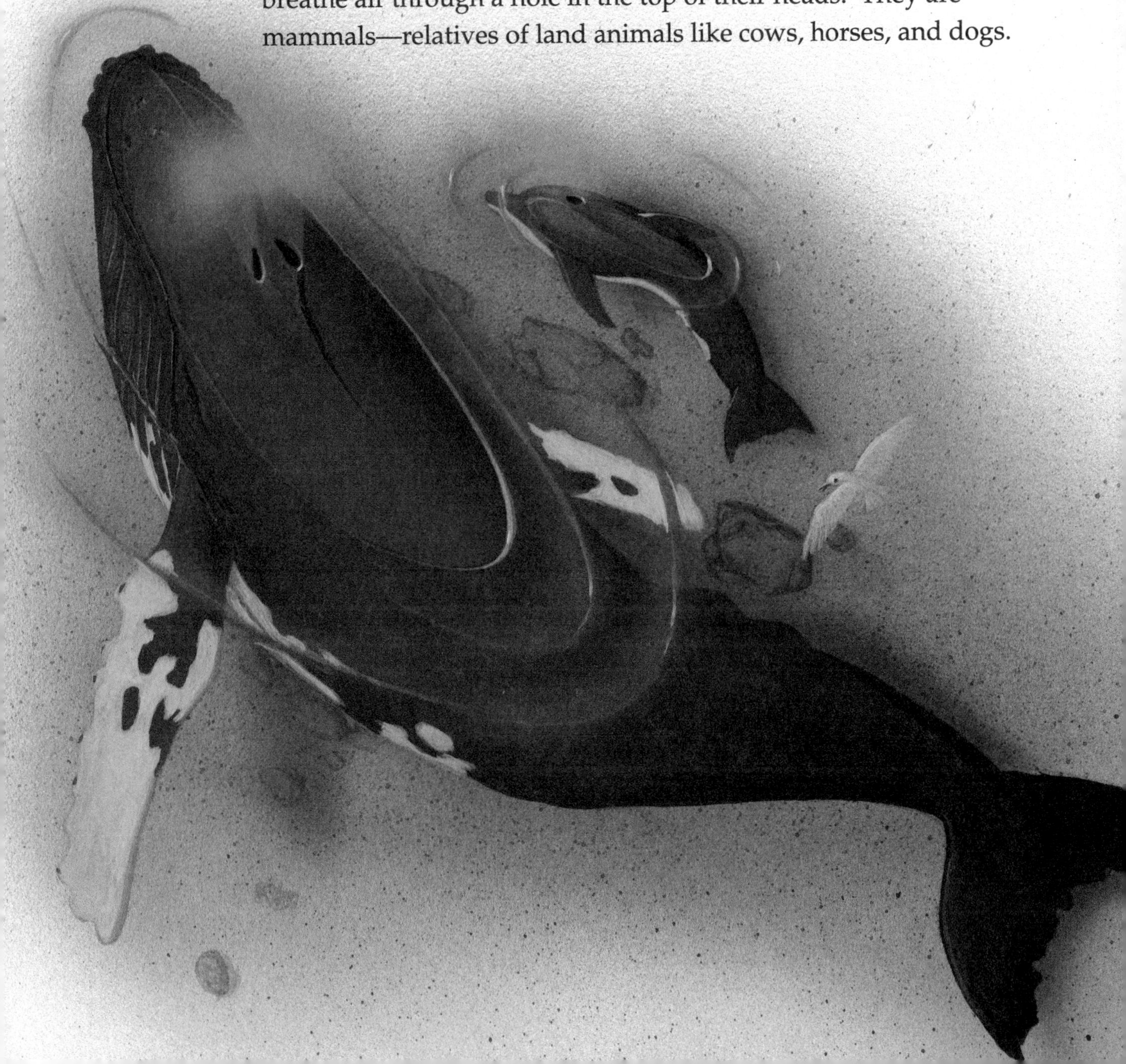

Whales are the biggest creatures in the sea. The biggest of all is the blue whale. It can be 100 feet long. That's bigger than the biggest dinosaur that ever lived! This is a fin whale. It's very big too — up to 80 feet long.

When a baby fin whale is born, it is already as big as a car! It drinks its mother's milk and grows even bigger. A young whale needs lots of food, and the cold seas near the North Pole are filled with fish and tiny sea creatures. So, in the late spring, the baby and its mother head north. They can swim thousands of miles in just a few weeks.

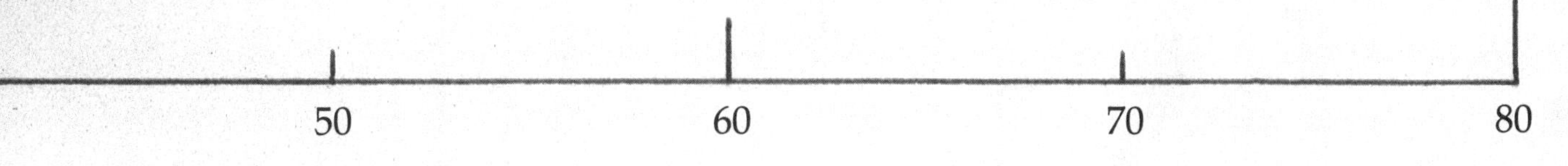

The fin whale has an unusual way of eating. It never chews its food. If you look inside the whale's mouth, you will see why. It has no teeth! Instead, it has strips of baleen. The baleen looks like a very thick scrub brush. When the whale slurps up a mouthful of water, tiny fish, shrimp, and other sea creatures get caught in its baleen.

The humpback is another big whale that has baleen instead of teeth. Not too many years ago, scientists learned that humpback whales "sing." The "song" of the whale is an eerie sound—sometimes high, sometimes low, part squeak, part rumble, part moan. It travels a long way under water. Why do humpbacks sing? Scientists aren't sure. They may be singing to attract mates. Or maybe they are just calling to one another.

The killer whale is also known as the orca. It is not a baleen whale. It has big, cone-shaped teeth. Orcas are the only whales that eat seals, penguins, dolphins, and other whales. They even attack whales that are bigger than they are!

Do humans have to worry about killer whales? No. They do not eat people. In fact, they can be very gentle with humans. And they are very smart. Killer whales are often the star performers in aquarium shows. They let people feed them by hand—and sometimes give them a big whale kiss!

The whale shark is the biggest fish in the ocean. It is not a whale at all, though, just a big, lazy shark that is almost as long as a trailer truck. It swims along, scooping up tiny sea creatures in its wide mouth. A whale shark can be a scary sight, especially if you are in a small sailboat. But whale sharks are really harmless.

Sharks have been living in the ocean since the time of the dinosaurs. There are more than 300 different kinds. Many of them are hunters. Hunter sharks will eat almost anything. Sometimes a shark will bite so hard that its teeth get stuck in its prey. This doesn't bother the shark! It keeps growing new teeth to replace the ones that fall out. In ten years, a shark can grow 20,000 teeth!

The great white shark is the biggest of the hunter sharks. It can weigh up to three tons.

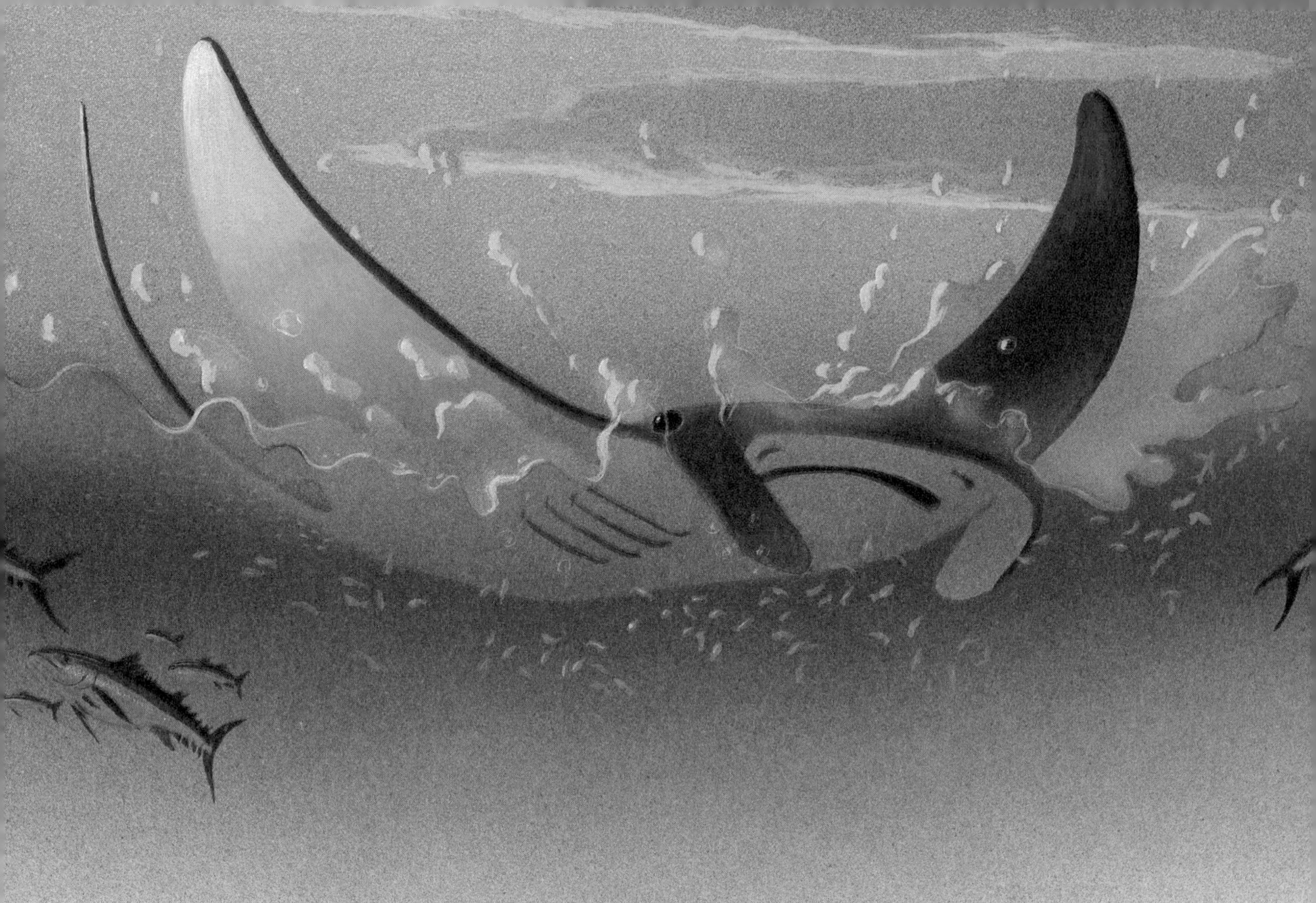

The ray is another fish that has lived in the ocean for millions of years. The manta is the biggest member of the ray family. Its mouth can be three feet wide! Mantas swim far out to sea. Every so often, a manta will leap out of the water and come down hard on its flat belly. *Thwack!* No one is sure why mantas do this. Some people think the manta is fishing. It pounds the water so hard that small fish nearby are knocked out. Then the manta can eat them.

Stingrays lie on the bottom in shallow water. Once in a while, a swimmer will step on a stingray by mistake. The ray lashes out with its tail. Getting stung by a stingray is no joke! A spike on the stingray's tail holds a poison that can make people sick.

A squid has eight regular arms and two extra-long arms called tentacles. All ten arms are covered with round, sticky cups. The squid uses these sticky cups to catch fish. Most squids are only one or two feet long. But there are giant squids living in the ocean. Some are as much as 40 feet long!

Many years ago, a sailor on a whaling ship saw a giant squid fighting with a whale. This sailor was lucky. Few people have ever seen a living giant squid. It is one of the most mysterious creatures in the sea.

The octopus is a shy cousin of the squid. Octopuses usually live in caves in shallow water near the shore. Sometimes the octopus will pile up rocks, shells, and even old rubber sandals in front of its cave home.

When a skin diver comes along, the octopus gets scared. A scared octopus will change color! If it is really frightened, it can shoot out a stream of ink. The ink makes it hard for the skin diver to see. In a flash, the octopus makes its escape.

The moray eel is the octopus's enemy. An eel is a kind of fish, but it looks more like a thick, slippery snake.

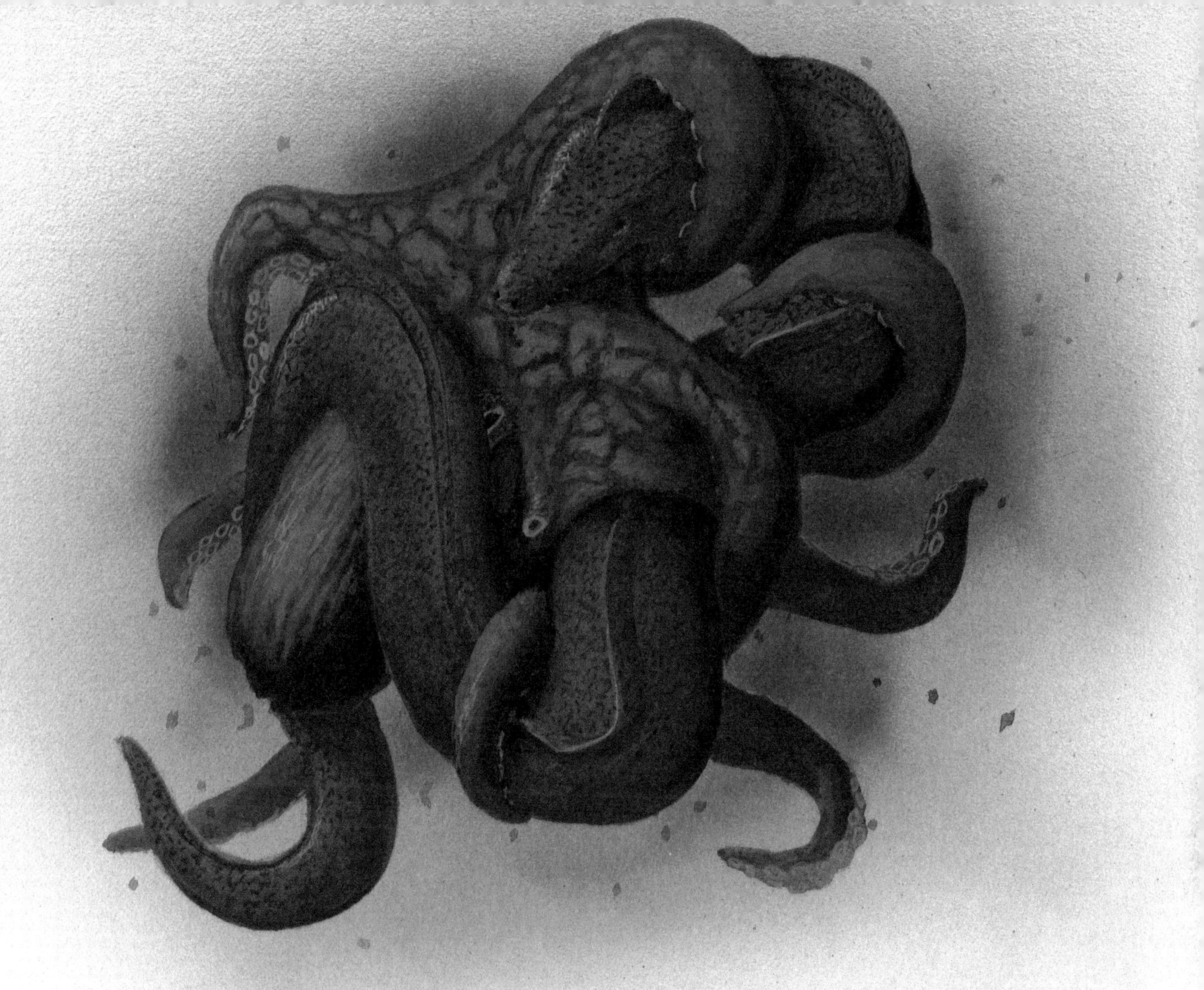

The moray eel hides inside caves and sunken ships. It peers out of the opening until an octopus swims by. Then it darts out and grabs the octopus!

Skin divers have to watch out for morays. These eels have very sharp teeth!

Coral is a kind of sea animal that looks like a plant. Many tiny corals growing together form a reef. The hard part of the reef is made up of the skeletons of millions of dead corals.

Small, brightly colored fish swim in and out of the coral. Crabs scurry underneath it. There are many good hiding places for octopuses and eels. Larger fish like sharks sometimes use the reef as a nursery. The young live there until they are able to survive in the open sea.

A young carpet shark is resting near the reef. This funny-looking shark has spotted skin and a fringe around its mouth. When it stays very still, it is almost impossible to see.

The sea anemone lives on coral reefs and underwater rocks. It looks like a flower with big, showy petals. But watch out! Those aren't petals. They are stinging tentacles. And that "bud" in the center of the anemone "flower" is really a mouth. After the anemone has poisoned a fish with its stinging tentacles, it opens its mouth and swallows the fish up.

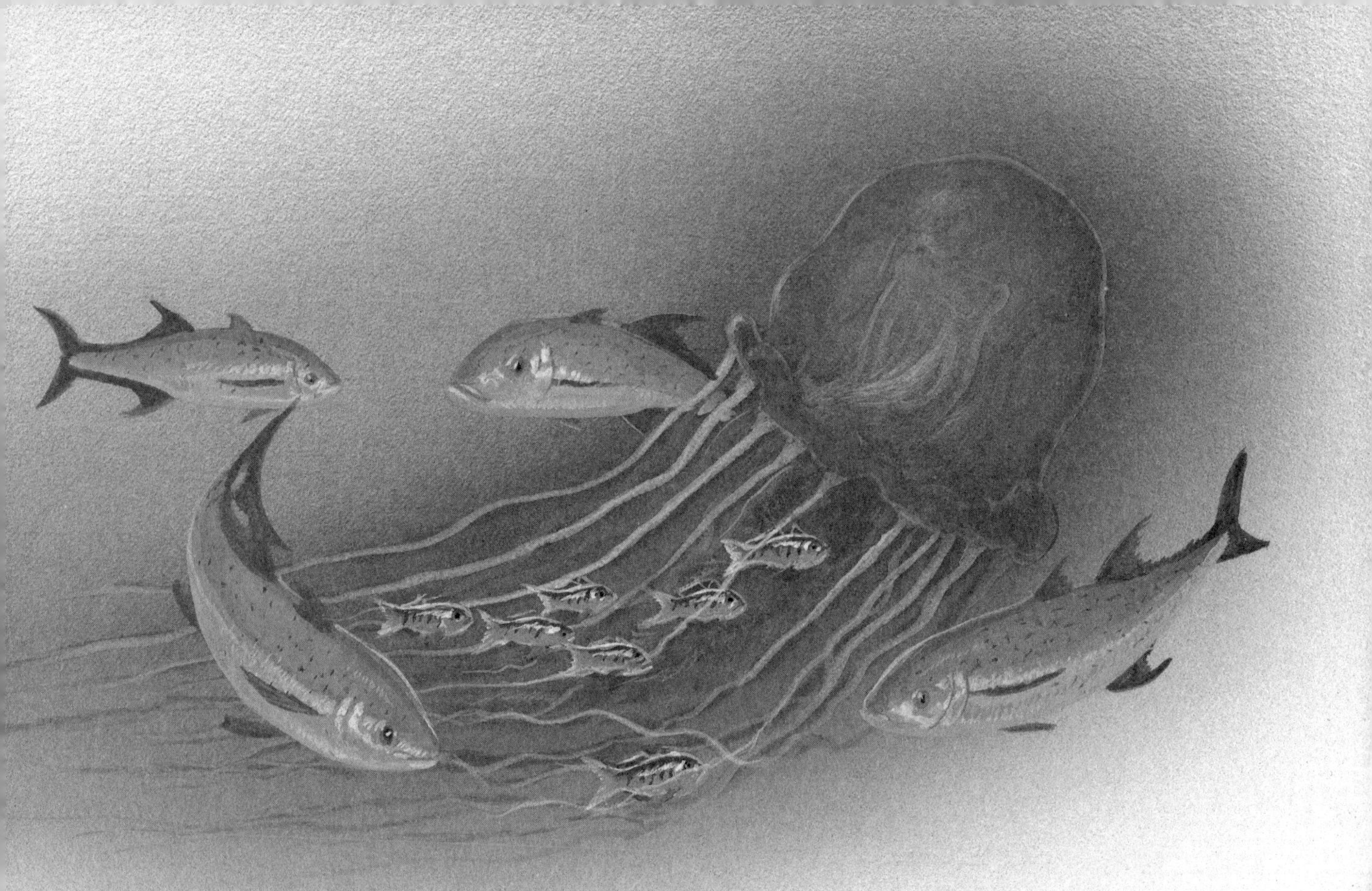

Jellyfish live in many parts of the ocean. Drifting along near the surface of the water, a jellyfish can look like a beautiful billowing parachute. But like anemones, jellyfish have stinging tentacles. Strangely, that doesn't stop some tiny fish from swimming nearby. The little fish stay close to the jellyfish for protection from big, hungry fish. The tentacles don't seem to bother them.

One kind of jellyfish, called a sea wasp, has tentacles that grow to be 30 feet long.

Thousands of feet down, the sea is cold and black. The fish that live here are often small, with rubbery bodies. Some have oversize mouths—like this gulper eel. Many have body parts that glow in the dark.

One of these deepwater fish is called an angler. It has a sort of fishing line growing out of its head. On the end of the line is a glowing light that attracts other fish. When one swims close, the angler springs into action. It swallows its prey whole.

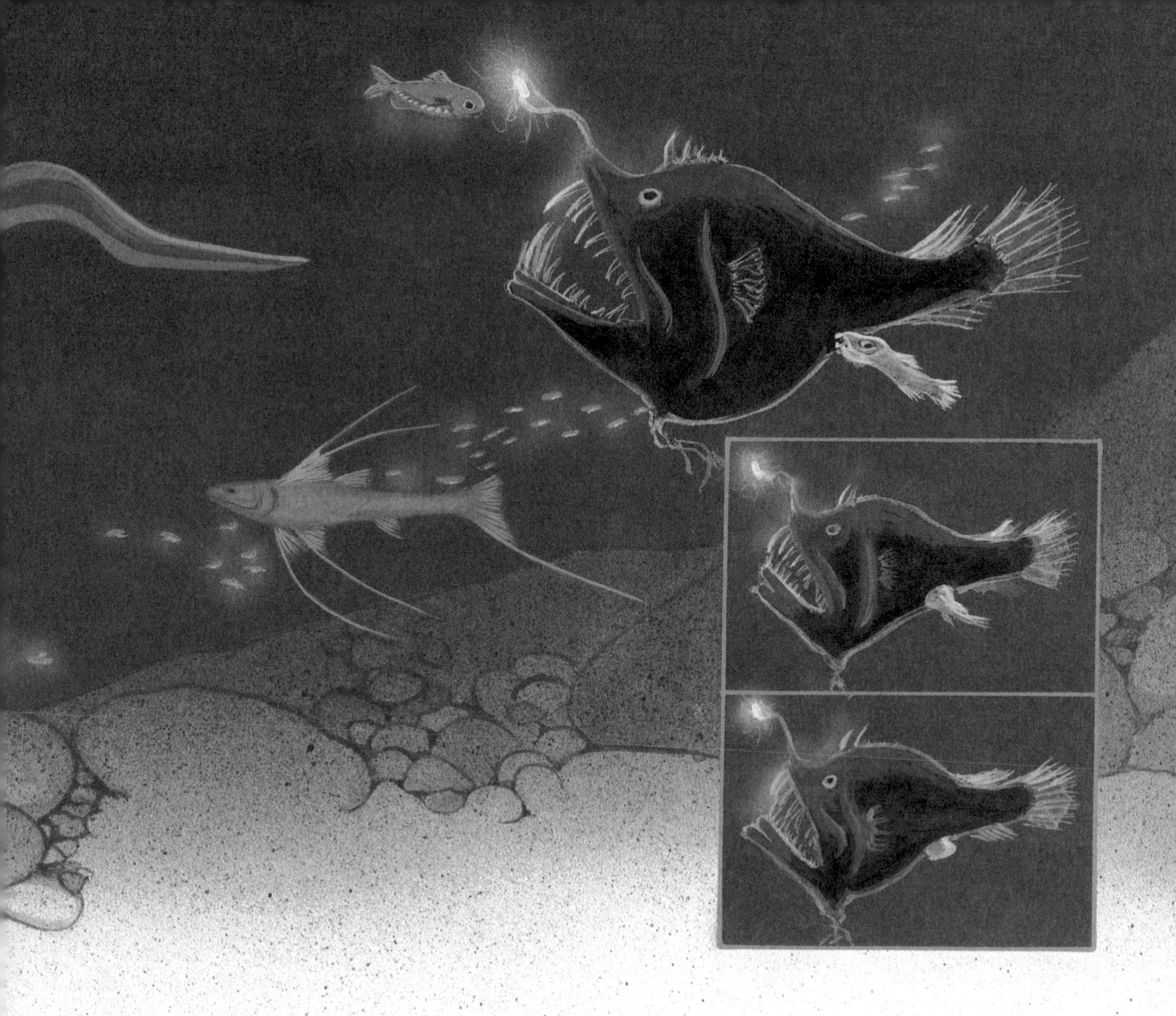

When a male angler fish finds a female, it bites the side of the female's body and hangs on. Then a strange thing happens. The male fish gets smaller and smaller. Soon nothing is left but a little lump. The male angler has become part of the female fish!

Robot submarines and even a few humans have gone down to the very deepest parts of the ocean. No one expected to find any living creatures there. But they did!

Some spots on the ocean floor are warmed by heat from the center of the earth. Animals can grow very large there. Big clams thrive in the warm water. Blind crabs scuttle across the sandy bottom. Bright red tube worms with no mouths or eyes live inside long, hollow tubes. These worms can be twelve feet long.

More people have rocketed into space than have visited the ocean depths. Scientists keep finding new sea creatures that do not even have names. The sea is still an unknown frontier, waiting to be explored.

INDEX

angler fish, 28-29

baleen, 10, 11
blue whale, 8

carpet shark, 25
clams, 30
coral, 24-25
crabs, 30

dolphins, 6-7

eels, 22, 24, 28

fin whale, 8-10

great white shark, 15
gulper eel, 28

humpback whale, 11

jellyfish, 27

killer whale, 12

manta ray, 16
moray eel, 22-23

octopus, 20-21, 24
orca, *see* killer whale

rays, 16-17
reef, 24-25

sea anemone, 26
sea wasp, 27
sharks, 14, 15, 24
"song," whale, 11
squid, 18
squid, giant, 18
stingray, 17

tentacles, 18, 26, 27
tube worms, 30

whales, 6-12, 18
whale shark, 14